164016 EN
Perfectly Poppy Snowy Blast

Jakubowski, Michele
ATOS BL 2.6
Points: 0.5

Perfectly POPPY

Snowy Blast

Story by Michele Jakubowski

Pictures by Erica-Jane Waters

Picture Window Books

Perfectly Poppy is published by Picture Window Books, a Capstone Imprint
1710 Roe Crest Drive, North Mankato, Minnesota 56003
www.capstonepub.com

Library of Congress Cataloging-in-Publication Data
Jakubowski, Michele, author.
Perfectly Poppy snowy blast / by Michele Jakubowski ; illustrated by Erica-Jane Waters.
pages cm. –– (Perfectly Poppy)
Summary: It is the first big snow of the winter and Poppy does not
want to play outside in the cold, but her mother insists.
ISBN 978-1-4795-2283-5 (hardcover) –– ISBN 978-1-4795-2357-3 (pbk.)
1. Snow––Juvenile fiction. 2. Outdoor recreation––Juvenile fiction. 3. Play––Juvenile fiction.
[1. Snow––Fiction. 2. Outdoor recreation––Fiction. 3. Play––Fiction.]
I. Waters, Erica-Jane, illustrator. II. Title. III. Title: Snowy blast.
PZ7.J153555Ph 2014
813.6––dc23
2013027853

Designers: Heather Kindseth Wutschke and Kristi Carlson

Printed in the United States of America in North Mankato, Minnesota.
042015   008805R

Table of Contents

Chapter 1

The Inside Day. 5

Chapter 2

Change of Plans 11

Chapter 3

The Snowball Fight. 18

Chapter 1

The Inside Day

On Saturday morning, Poppy woke up and looked out the window. She knew it was going to snow, but she didn't know it was going to snow so much!

"I know just what I want to do today," Poppy said.

Poppy hopped down the stairs and into the kitchen.

"Good morning, Poppy," her mom said. "Would you like oatmeal with raisins?"

"You know it!" Poppy said.

Poppy's older brother, Nolan, jumped up from the table.

"I finished my breakfast," he said. "I'm going outside now."

"Don't forget your hat and gloves!" yelled Poppy's mom as Nolan rushed out the door.

Once she finished her oatmeal,

Poppy was ready for her perfect day.

And unlike Nolan, her perfect day did

not involve going outside in the cold.

Just last week Poppy had slipped

on ice and hurt her arm. She did not

want that to happen again.

Poppy grabbed her favorite fuzzy
blanket. She found a spot on the
couch near the fireplace. Then she
clicked on the TV.

"Don't you look comfy," said Poppy's mom.

"I sure am!" Poppy told her.

Poppy pulled up her blanket.

"Nolan's crazy," she said. "Who would want to play outside in the snow and cold?"

Chapter 2
Change of Plans

Poppy watched TV for a while. But after a few shows, Poppy was bored.

"I'm bored," she complained to her mom.

"You can always go outside,"

her mom said.

"No way. I guess I'll just read,"

Poppy said.

After finishing her favorite book,

it was time for lunch. Nolan came in

to eat.

"Why are you still in your pajamas?" he asked. "You should come outside and play. It is so fun!"

Nolan's cheeks were pink. His nose was bright red. That didn't look like much fun to Poppy.

"No way," Poppy said. "After lunch I'm going to watch some more TV."

"It would be good for you to go outside and play," said Poppy's mom.

"No thanks, Mom," Poppy said.

She got up from the table and headed for the couch.

"I don't think so," Poppy's mom said. She turned Poppy toward the stairs. "Go get dressed in warm clothes. You need to get some fresh air and exercise young lady."

Poppy marched slowly up the
stairs. She didn't want to go outside.
This was not part of her perfect day.

Poppy took a long time to get
dressed. Her mom made her put on
a hat, gloves, and a scarf.

When she went outside, Poppy

stood in the snow with her arms

folded. Her mom made her go outside.

She couldn't make her have fun.

Chapter 3

The Snowball Fight

After a few minutes of pouting,

Poppy felt a snowball hit her back.

Poppy didn't like playing in the

snow, and she really didn't like being

hit with a snowball!

"Got you!" Nolan shouted. He was making another snowball to throw.

Poppy scooped up some snow and made a snowball. She quickly threw it. The snowball hit Nolan on the arm.

Nolan looked surprised. "Wow, Poppy! Nice shot! You can be on my team."

"Team? Who else is out here?" Poppy asked.

"Everyone!" Nolan said.

"You should have said something! You know I hate to miss out on fun things," Poppy said.

"Now you know. Let's get busy," Nolan said.

Poppy followed Nolan behind a big tree. They made a huge pile of snowballs. Then they made a plan. Poppy was getting excited.

"I'll run out first," Nolan said.

"You follow me and hit the others
with snowballs."

"We can call our plan 'the snowy
blast,'" Poppy said with excitement.

"Awesome! Ready?" Nolan asked.

"Yes!" Poppy yelled.

Nolan and Poppy made a great team. Poppy was good at throwing. Nolan was really quick. Together they dodged snowballs and took out the other teams.

After a while the other kids had

to go home.

"Do you want to go inside?"

Nolan asked.

"Not yet," Poppy said.

Nolan smiled. "Want to make a
snowman?"

"I've got a better idea!" Poppy
said. "Let's make a giant trophy
out of snow. After all, we were the
winners of the snowball fight."

And even though it was cold outside, Poppy had a warm feeling inside.

"Now THIS is the perfect day," Poppy said with a smile as she started to make their snow trophy.

"It sure is," Nolan said.

Poppy's New Words

I learned so many new words today! I made sure to write them down so I could use them again.

bored (BORD) — not interested

comfy (KUHM-fee) — relaxed

complained (KUHM-playnd) — said you were unhappy about something

dodged (DOJD) — avoided something by moving quickly

involve (in-VOLV) — to include something as a necessary part

pouting (POUT-ing) — to push out your lip when you are angry or disappointed

Poppy's Ponders

After my day in the snow, I had some time to think. Here are some of my questions and thoughts from the day.

1. Do you like to play inside or outside? Why?

2. Watching TV is fun, but why is it important to go outside and play?

3. I didn't want to go outside, but once I did I had a lot of fun. Write about a time when you did something you didn't want to do.

4. Nolan and I did lots of fun things in the snow. Write about your favorite thing to do in the snow.

Cold Day Menu

When it's cold outside, I like a lot of warm food to fill my belly. Here are my favorite meals for cold days.

Breakfast:

Oatmeal with raisins and milk

Lunch:

Chicken noodle soup, a grilled cheese sandwich, an apple, and milk

Snack:

Hot chocolate with marshmallows and banana bread

Dinner:

Lasagna with garlic bread, a garden salad, and milk

Make a menu of your favorite cold day foods. Then help your mom or dad go grocery shopping and make the meals. Yum!

Snow Day Fun

Once I went outside, I found lots of fun things to do in the snow. Here is a list of snow activities for you. Dress warm and try something new!

- build a snowman or an entire snow family

- make a snow angel

- build a snow fort

- throw snowballs

- make a snow castle (instead of a sand castle)

- help shovel

- go sledding

About the Author

Raised in the Chicago suburb of Hoffman Estates, Michele Jakubowski has the teachers in her life to thank for her love of reading and writing. While writing has always been a passion for Michele, she believes it is the books she has read throughout the years, and the teachers who assigned them, that have made her the storyteller she is today. Michele lives in Powell, Ohio, with her husband, John, and their children, Jack and Mia.

About the Illustrator

Erica-Jane Waters grew up in the beautiful Northern Irish countryside, where her imagination was ignited by the local folklore and fairy tales. She now lives in Oxfordshire, England, with her young family. Erica writes and illustrates children's books and creates art for magazines, greeting cards, and various other projects.

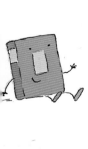

Distributed to Schools and Libraries
in the United States by
ENCYCLOPAEDIA BRITANNICA EDUCATIONAL CORP.
310 S. Michigan Avenue
Chicago, Illinois 60604

Library of Congress Cataloging-in-Publication Data

A Little Book of friendship / illustrated by Penny Dann
p. cm.
Summary: Quotations about friendship
taken from famous sources.
ISBN 1-56766-095-9
1. Friendship - Quotations, maxims, etc.
Juvenile literature.
[1 Friendship - Quotations, maxims, etc.]
I. Dann, Penny, ill.
BJ1533.F8L57 1993   93-12918
177'.6 - dc20   CIP/AC

A Little Book of FRiENDSHiP

Pictures by Penny Dann

The only way to have a friend
is to be a friend.

Ralph Waldo Emerson

to friends, old & new
P.D.

Everyone possesses the power to enrich life. Our effectiveness, however, depends upon our ability to openly express our thoughts. This little book is intended to help us do that. The following pages contain a variety of thoughts concerning friendship. Read the words carefully. Think of ways they can enrich your life. Then, share your thoughts about friendship – and any other subject under the sun – with your friends.

Every person has a heart, and if you can reach it, you can make a difference.

Uli Derickson

Choose an author as you
choose a friend.

Wentworth Dillon

Friends do not live in harmony merely, as some say, but in melody.

Henry David Thoreau

Friendship is a
sheltering tree.
Samuel Taylor Coleridge

Love thy neighbor as thyself.

One friend in a lifetime is much; two are many; three are hardly possible.

Henry Adams

Some of my best friends are children. In fact,
all of my best friends are children.

J. D. Salinger

Tell me who admires and loves you, and I will tell you who you are.

Charles Augustin Sainte-Beuve

A companion loves some agreeable qualities which a person may possess, but a friend loves the whole person.

James Boswell

Animals are such agreeable friends –
they ask no questions, they pass no criticisms.
George Eliot (Mary Ann Evans)

My friend is the person who will tell me my faults, in private.

Ibn Gabirol

Your friend is the person who knows all about you and still likes you.

Elbert Hubbard

How I like to be liked,
and what I do to be liked!

Charles Lamb

That is best – to laugh with someone because you both think the same things are funny.

Gloria Vanderbilt

Love is a gift we all have to give that costs nothing.... and means everything.

Mary Roberts Rinehart

The better part of one's life consists of one's friendships.

Abraham Lincoln

The bird a nest, the spider a web, the human friendship.

William Blake

Oh darling it's just perfect!

One's best friend is in the mirror.

Jewish saying

First of all, be a friend to yourself.

Anonymous

The greatest gift you can give another is the purity of your attention.

Dr. Richard Moss

You know how I feel...you listen to how I think... you understand...you are my friend.

Kahlil Gibran

Sooner or later you've heard about
all your best friends have to say. Then comes
the tolerance of real love.

Ned Rorem

Yes'm, old friends is always best, 'less you can catch a new one that's fit to make an old one out of.

Sarah Orne Jewett

The differences between
friends cannot but reinforce
their friendship.

Mao Tse-Tung

Love conquers all things.

Virgil

The only safe way to destroy an enemy
is to make him your friend.

P. Dormann

Do good and disappear.

Genevieve Hennet de Goutel.